STEP INTO READING® will help your child get there. The program offers five steps to reading success. Each step includes fun stories and colorful art or photographs. In addition to original fiction and books with favorite characters, there are Step into Reading Non-Fiction Readers, Phonics Readers and Boxed Sets, Sticker Readers, and Comic Readers—a complete literacy program with something to interest every child.

Learning to Read, Step by Step!

Ready to Read   Preschool–Kindergarten
• big type and easy words • rhyme and rhythm • picture clues
For children who know the alphabet and are eager to begin reading.

Reading with Help   Preschool–Grade 1
• basic vocabulary • short sentences • simple stories
For children who recognize familiar words and sound out new words with help.

Reading on Your Own   Grades 1–3
• engaging characters • easy-to-follow plots • popular topics
For children who are ready to read on their own.

Reading Paragraphs   Grades 2–3
• challenging vocabulary • short paragraphs • exciting stories
For newly independent readers who read simple sentences with confidence.

Ready for Chapters   Grades 2–4
• chapters • longer paragraphs • full-color art
For children who want to take the plunge into chapter books but still like colorful pictures.

STEP INTO READING® is designed to give every child a successful reading experience. The grade levels are only guides; children will progress through the steps at their own speed, developing confidence in their reading. The F&P Text Level on the back cover serves as another tool to help you choose the right book for your child.

Remember, a lifetime love of reading starts with a single step!

Copyright © 2022 by Kristen Bell
Cover art and interior illustrations by Daniel Wiseman

All rights reserved. Published in the United States by Random House Children's Books,
a division of Penguin Random House LLC, New York.

Step into Reading, Random House, and the Random House colophon are registered trademarks
of Penguin Random House LLC.

Visit us on the Web!
StepIntoReading.com
rhcbooks.com

Educators and librarians, for a variety of teaching tools, visit us at RHTeachersLibrarians.com

Library of Congress Control Number: 2021945585
ISBN 978-0-593-43444-4 (trade) — ISBN 978-0-593-43445-1 (lib. bdg.) —
ISBN 978-0-593-43446-8 (ebook)

Printed in the United States of America
10 9 8 7 6 5 4 3 2 1

This book has been officially leveled by using the F&P Text Level Gradient™ Leveling System.

Let's Go, Bike!

by Kristen Bell and Benjamin Hart
illustrations by Daniel Wiseman

Random House 🏠 New York

Penny Purple

has a new purple bike.

Today she will

take a ride.

Do you want to
know where?
Good!

Purple people are curious.

Penny's neighbor Goldie
loves to garden.
Penny loves to ask Goldie
questions.

Goldie puts on
her purple skates.

Penny sees
her neighbor Emma.
Penny likes to sing
funny songs with Emma.

Emma hops on
her purple skateboard.

Penny sees

her neighbor Max.

Today Max is taking
laundry off the line.

Penny likes to help Max
with his work.
It makes her feel purple.

It is hard work.
But it smells great!

Max straps on
his purple backpack.

Penny sees
her friend Mateo.

He is playing with his dog.

Penny uses her voice
to call out to him.

Mateo grabs

his dog's purple leash.

Everyone is going
to a purple place.
That is a place where
they can be themselves.
A purple place
is a happy place!
Where is it?

It is at the bottom
of a hill.

Ready?

Set.

Go!

The bike goes fast.

The skates go fast.

The skateboard
goes fast.

Everyone goes fast.

What do they do

at the bottom of the hill?

They have a picnic!

Picnics feel purple . . .

. . . when each friend brings something to share!